This Book Belongs To..

....

....

....

Made in the USA
Monee, IL
05 June 2022

97491547R00056